D0452638

For Mum and Dad – Susan Chandler

For Laura and Adrian – Sanja Rešček

Editor: Ruth Symons
Designer: Anna Lubecka
Editorial Director: Victoria Garrard
Art Director: Laura Roberts-Jensen

First published in the UK in 2015 by QED Publishing
A Quarto Group company, The Old Brewery, 6 Blundell Street, London, N7 9BH

www. qed-publishing.co.uk

A catalogue record for this book is available from the British Library.

ISBN 978 1 78171 661 8

Printed in China

The Greedy Rainbow

Susan Chandler

SanjaReščček

QED Publishing

Monkey sat at the top of the
highest tree in the forest.

Looking around, he
spied a tiny rainbow
in the leaves.

"What a pretty little rainbow!" Monkey said.

"I will take you down to meet my friends."

The rainbow bounced towards him.

"Wrap yourself around my tail," said Monkey.

Then he started climbing
down towards the forest floor.

While they were climbing down,
something strange started happening!

As the rainbow went past,
the red flowers and
green leaves started
losing their colour.

Worse still –
Monkey's golden
fur was fading too!

But Monkey didn't notice. He was too busy swinging from branch to branch.

He didn't see the berries' red colour fading.

He didn't notice when the orange snake and yellow parrot lost their colours.

As the rainbow went past, the green leaves, blue sky, indigo dragonfly and violet butterfly all grew dull and lost their colours.

At last, Monkey reached the forest floor.

"Come and meet this little rainbow!" he called to his friends.

But the rainbow wasn't little
any more! It had grown
bigger and heavier.

In fact, it was so big
that it reached the
tops of the trees!

The animals gathered around, but the toucan got too close to the rainbow. Her magnificent beak suddenly lost its bright colours.

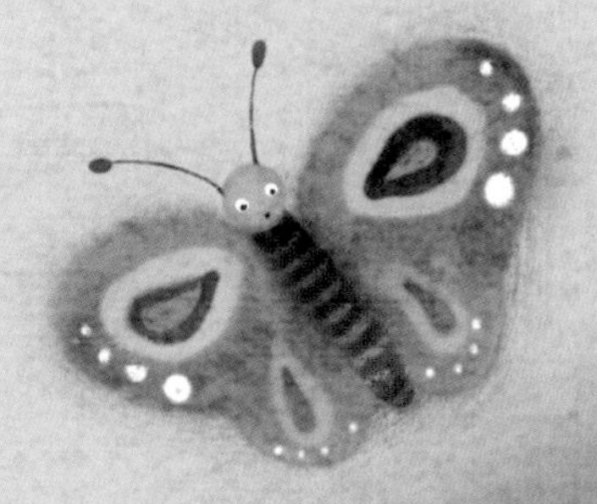

"Keep back," Monkey warned.

But it was too late. The rainbow was eating all of the colours!

It GOBBLED and MUNCHED and *SLURPED* until...

...the entire rainforest was grey!

The animals were very sad.

"Look what you've done!" cried Monkey.

"You've been *so* greedy that you've eaten all of the colours. Now there aren't any left for us to enjoy."

The rainbow gazed down at the rainforest. It wasn't as beautiful without its dazzling colours.

Then the rainbow looked at Monkey and his friends.

It saw how unhappy they
were and it felt very bad.

If only it hadn't
been so selfish.

The rainbow sighed and sniffed,
then burst into tears!

Big wet splodges of red, orange, yellow, green, blue, indigo and violet splashed onto the forest soaking everything.

As the rainbow cried, it shrank and drifted high into the forest canopy. It was glad that it had shared the colours with the rainforest.

And of course, everything and
everyone got their colours back...

...just not the same colours they had before!

Next steps

Could the children guess what the story would be about by looking at the front cover? Did the title help?

Ask the children if they have ever seen a rainbow. Had it been raining, or did it rain afterwards? Rainbows only appear when it is sunny and raining at the same time!

The rainbow in this story took all the jungle colours for itself. Can the children think of a time when they have been selfish? Can they think of something that they enjoy sharing? What made the rainbow give all the colours back?

Ask the children to write down all seven colours of the rainbow. How many red animals can they see in the book? How many orange animals are there? Can the children find an animal for every colour of the rainbow?

Discuss what the world would be like if everything were grey. How would this make the children feel? Can the children think of any animals that are grey already?

Ask the children if they have a favourite colour. Why do they like that colour?

Discuss the end of the book. How do the animals look with their new colours? If the children could change the colour of one animal, what would it be and why? Ask them to draw and colour their idea.